THIS CANDLEWICK BOOK BELONGS TO:

_____

_____

_____

_____

TUGBOAT MARY

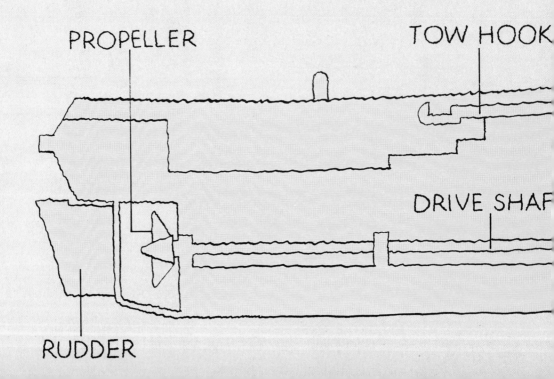

PROPELLER

TOW HOOK

DRIVE SHAF

RUDDER

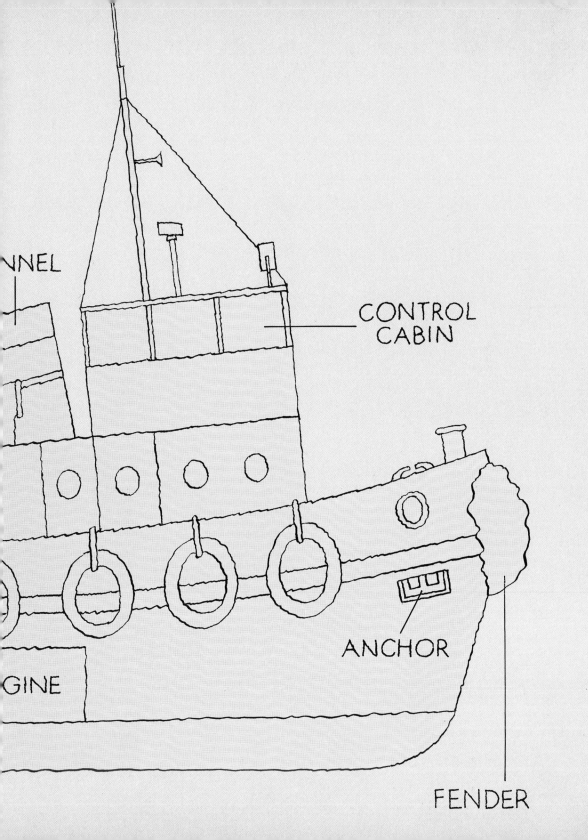

NNEL

CONTROL
CABIN

ANCHOR

GINE

FENDER

First U.S. edition 1995

Library of Congress Cataloging-in-Publication Data

Blanchard, Arlene.
The tugboat / Arlene Blanchard ;
illustrated by Tony Wells. — 1st U.S. ed.
Summary: Describes the daily routine
of a tugboat named Mary.
ISBN 1-56402-524-1
[1. Tugboats — Fiction.]
I. Wells, Tony, ill.   II. Title.
PZ7.B592Tu   1995
[E]—dc20   94-25705

2 4 6 8 10 9 7 5 3 1

Printed in Hong Kong

The pictures in this book were done in gouache and ink.

Candlewick Press
2067 Massachusetts Avenue
Cambridge, Massachusetts 02140

The Tugboat

Arlene Blanchard
illustrated by Tony Wells

CANDLEWICK PRESS
CAMBRIDGE, MASSACHUSETTS

Pat, Bob, and Rick are the crew
of the tugboat Mary. All day long
Mary chugs in and out of the harbor.

She is busy meeting the big ships
and towing them through the narrow
harbor entrance to their berths.

The big ships stop their engines, but they still keep moving. Mary has the hard job of turning them.

Today she is bringing in a cargo ship
carrying iron ore from Brazil.
Bob and Rick watch the towline.

A passenger ship comes in, full of
people on vacation. Mary helps to push
her into the berth where she will anchor.

The ship is tied securely and Mary chugs away. Some of the people wave. Bob and Rick wave back.

An urgent message comes over the
radio. An oil tanker is stuck on
a sandbank.

All tugs are needed to help pull
her off. The weather forecast
is very bad.

Pat steers Mary out toward
the sandbank. Bob and Rick
check their gear.

They see the grounded tanker.
Other tugs are hurrying
to the scene.

At high tide all the tugs do their best, but the tanker will not budge. Big waves bump her up and down.

Now they must wait for the next tide.
But that will be a smaller one.
They need to lighten her load.

A smaller tanker comes to take off some of her cargo of oil. That will make her float more easily.

Mary must pull the smaller tanker alongside the larger one. Pat steers very carefully because the sea is rough.

The stranded ship pumps oil through
a pipe into the second tanker.
Mary and another tug stand by.

The pumping takes a long time.
Mary's crew is very tired. Then
oil starts to leak from the pipe.

An oil slick is forming on the water.
Mary has spraying gear on board.
Bob and Rick start to rig the booms.

Pat takes Mary through the slick.
The booms spray detergent on the
sea and the slick begins to break up.

At last it is high tide again.
The sea is calmer now. The tugs
are secured to the big tanker.

Pat listens to the messages on his radio.
Everyone waits. The tanker's captain
gives the order, "Full steam ahead!"

"Full steam ahead," says Pat at Mary's wheel. The little tugs heave together. The big tanker's engines throb.

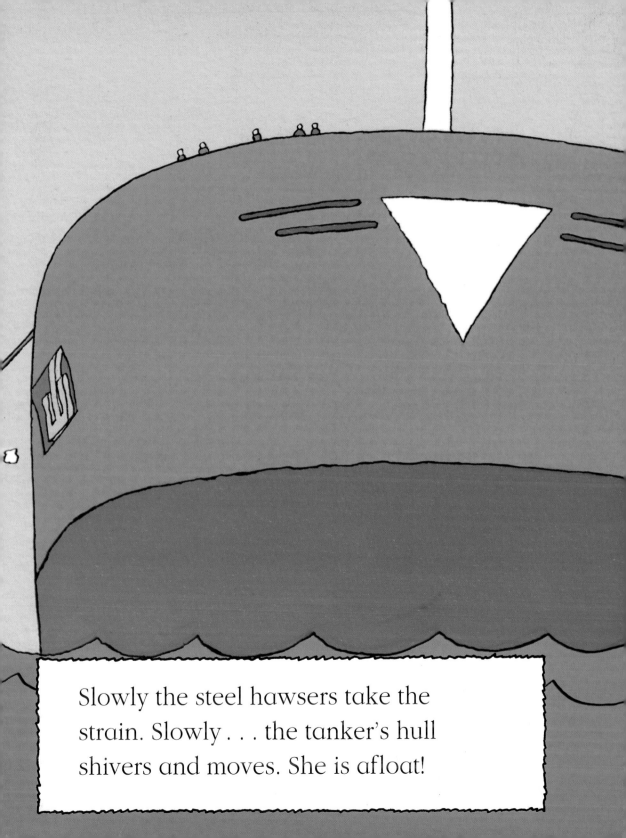

Slowly the steel hawsers take the strain. Slowly . . . the tanker's hull shivers and moves. She is afloat!

Other tugs will escort the damaged ship into port. Mary has done her job. Pat turns her bow toward home.

Pat, Bob, and Rick drink their mugs of hot tea. "Three cheers for Mary! Thank you, brave little tug!"

TUGBOAT MARY

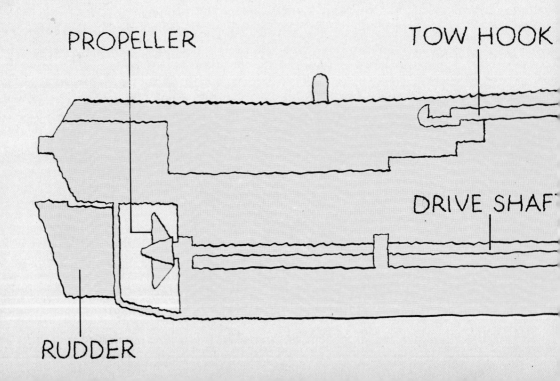

PROPELLER

TOW HOOK

DRIVE SHAFT

RUDDER

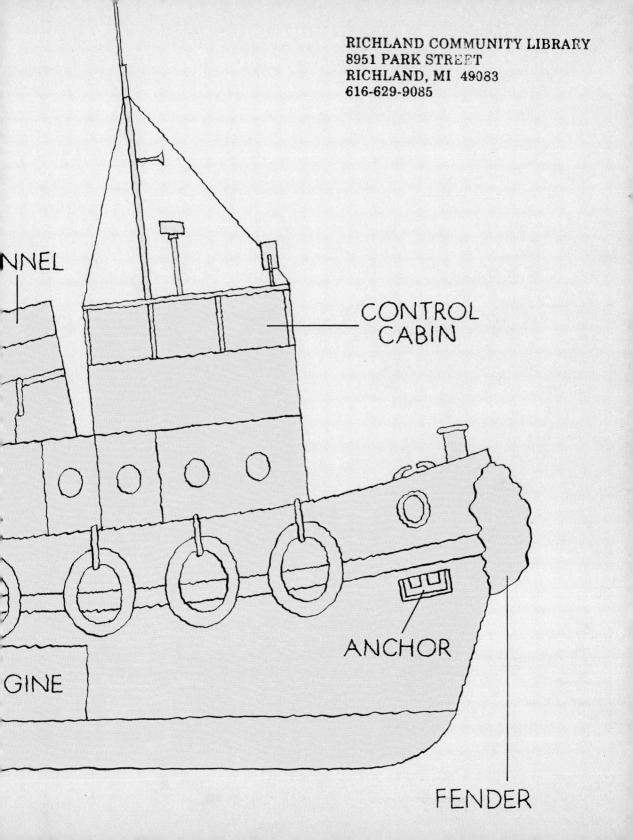

NNEL

CONTROL
CABIN

ANCHOR

GINE

FENDER

ARLENE BLANCHARD and TONY WELLS are the parents of two grown children. They collect antique toys and children's books and write books for children as a team.